MARVEL
ULTIMATE SPIDER-MAN

SPIDER-MAN
AND HIS AMAZING FRIENDS

written by John Sazaklis
designed by Can2 Design Group

MARVEL
marvelkids.com
© 2016 MARVEL

studio fun
A READER'S DIGEST COMPANY

White Plains, New York • Montréal, Québec • Bath, United Kingdom

Hi, my name is Peter Parker. It's another sunny day here in New York City and I'm on my way to school—just like the rest of the kids. I just tend to travel with a little more style—like swinging across the skyline as your friendly neighborhood Spider-Man!

That's right. This teenager is also a wall-crawling Super Hero! It all happened after I was bitten by a genetically altered spider which gave me spiderlike powers. Since then, I've been trying to juggle fighting bad guys and getting good grades. It isn't easy.

Luckily, I have awesome people in my life, like my best buds, Mary Jane and Harry, and my loving Aunt May, to help balance it out.

Other kids I know start their day with orange juice. ME? I get yelled at by a digital one-hundred-foot-tall cranky pants. I'm out here alone every day trying my best at this. It's not like they teach super-heroing in high school.

He is an orphan who lives with his loving Aunt May and Uncle Ben.

SPIDER-MAN IS A WALL-CRAWLING MENACE! AS LONG AS J. JONAH JAMESON IS CEO OF DAILY BUGLE COMMUNICATIONS, I SWEAR THAT THIS WILL BE THE LAST WE SEE OF THAT MASKED MISCREANT!

AND A GOOD MORNING TO YOU TOO, J. JONAH LOUDMOUTH!

When Uncle Ben was murdered by a criminal, Peter vowed to avenge him as Spider-Man.

3

Peter has expert knowledge in the areas of science, chemistry, physics, biology, engineering, mathematics, and mechanics.

I have plenty to do before first period—like getting to Romita's Bakery to pick up a cake for Aunt May. Uh-oh! Looks like someone is in trouble!

A police cruiser skids along the street with a sticky substance plastered across its windshield. It flips over and hurtles toward the bakery. Thinking quickly, I shoot my web fluid and catch the car in a net before it's too late.

SPLAT!

CRASH!

I'M STARTING TO THINK JAMESON'S WRONG ABOUT YOU, SPIDER-MAN!

SPREAD THE WORD, CHIEF!

With his talents, Peter creates his own Super Hero suit, as well as mechanical web shooters.

I swing toward an armored truck nearby. The back door has been blown off and the wheels are trapped in the same sticky substance that is on the police cruiser. A man steps out of the truck.

Spider-Man's web shooters are located on his wrists. They shoot an advanced web-fluid adhesive in many forms, including ropelike strands and netting.

HIYA, BUG BRAIN! I KNEW THAT WOULD DRAW YOU OUT.

OH, GREAT. IT'S THE TRAPSTER!

The Trapster appeared as Paste-Pot Pete in *Strange Tales* #104, and then as Trapster in *Fantastic Four* #38 (May 1965).

I've only been Spider-Man for a year, and already I've fought this glue stick three times! He doesn't seem to get the hint that crime doesn't pay. Oh well, here's hoping the fourth time is a charm.

The Trapster aims his glue gun and fires a stream of sealant at me. Thanks to my enhanced abilities, I evade the gooey glue with ease. In a flash, I deliver a devastating punch that sends this adhesive adversary across the street and into the side of a car.

CRUNCH!

I'M NOT FINISHED WITH YOU YET, SPIDER-MAN. MY NEXT STICKY TRICK IS A REAL BLAST!

BOOM! BOOM!

Trapster pulls out two armed glue grenades and hurls them in my direction. Batter up! I kick each one to opposite ends of the street where they detonate on impact.

His real name is Peter Petruski.

Unfortunately, the Trapster's third grenade catches me off guard, trapping me in a gob of glue. Oof! Guess my Spider-Sense is on the fritz. It's totally gross.

He constructed a special handgun that could project his paste formula without clogging.

ALLOW ME TO RETURN THE FAVOR!

I fire a wad of web fluid straight into the barrel of Trapster's weapon. The trigger jams, causing all his glue gear to explode—coating the villain in extrastrong sealant.

THWIP!

THE GOOD THING ABOUT YOUR GLUE IS THAT IT DRIES FAST AND HOLDS FOREVER!

After pulling myself free, I finally confront the Trapster. Suddenly, the sticky scoundrel's eyes go wide. A dark shadow covers the entire city block. I look up to see the S.H.I.E.L.D. Helicarrier hovering really low above the city.

A one-eyed man in a leather trench coat approaches me. It is Nick Fury, sensational superspy and director of S.H.I.E.L.D.

LOOK AROUND YOU, KID. WE GOTTA TALK.

DID I DO THAT?

YOU MAY HAVE STOPPED THE BAD GUY, BUT YOU MADE A MESS. CAPTAIN AMERICA WOULD HAVE HANDLED TRAPSTER IN FIVE SECONDS WITHOUT THE DAMAGE.

HEY, I DID A GOOD JOB!

I slowly take in my surrounding and realize that everyone is reeling from the aftermath of my tussle with the Trapster. A mother is pulling her stuck kid from the lamppost, a squad car is glued to the ground, and the officers are trying to unstick a police horse!

WHAT IF I TOLD YOU I COULD HELP YOU REACH YOUR ULTIMATE POTENTIAL?

IF YOU'RE SELLING SOMETHING, I'M TAPPED OUT 'TIL PAYDAY.

His first appearance was in the comic book *Sgt. Fury and His Howling Commandos* # 1 (May 1963).

I am not in the mood to have some spooky spy criticize my crime-fighting skills. I turn my back to walk away. Fury is starting to freak me out.

WITH S.H.I.E.L.D. TRAINING AND A TECH UPGRADE, YOU COULD BE THE NEXT CAP OR IRON MAN. WHAT DO YOU SAY?

UM...I'M NOT SUPPOSED TO TALK TO STRANGERS, SO, SEE YA!

By the time I swing all the way to Midtown High, change out of my Spidey suit, and run to my locker, it's already lunchtime. Mary Jane is waiting for me.

MJ is a student interested in journalism who wants to work for J. Jonah Jameson. She says her big ticket is an exclusive interview with Spider-Man—if she could only find him. Thankfully, she doesn't know he's standing right in front of her!

WHERE HAVE YOU BEEN ALL MORNING?

SORRY, THE BUS BROKE DOWN.

In the cafeteria, MJ and I sit with our friend, Harry. I try to talk about normal school things, but all of a sudden my Spider-Sense tingles!

UH-OH! TROUBLE.

A split second before the cafeteria wall explodes, I leap out of my seat to shield my friends. Three costumed figures enter. I recognize them immediately. They are the Wizard, master of high-tech gadgets, Klaw, the villain made of solid sound, and Thundra, warrior woman from the future.

Harry Osborn and Peter became best friends when Peter's bike broke down in the rain and Harry gave him a ride in his limo.

WE ARE THE FRIGHTFUL FOUR.

UH...THERE'S ONLY THREE OF YOU.

BEFORE OUR COMRADE, THE TRAPSTER, WAS CAPTURED, HE TOLD US THAT SPIDER-MAN ATTENDS THIS SCHOOL. KLAW, MAKE THEM LISTEN TO REASON.

The Klaw activates his sonic cannon, causing the room to reverberate. The foundation rumbles and the walls crack. Students cover their ears and cry out in pain. I yell at the villains, catching their attention.

Klaw's first appearance was in *Fantastic Four* #53 (August 1966).

HEY! I'VE GOT SOMETHING TO SAY!!

TWO WORDS: FOOD FIGHT!

I pick up a nearby lunch tray and chuck it at the Wizard, knocking him off balance. SPLAT!

This incites the most epic food fight in the history of Midtown High. Kids are throwing food at the Klaw and Thundra, creating just the diversion I needed to find a hiding spot and change into my Spidey suit.

CRASH!

SMACK!

Thundra's first appearance was in *Fantastic Four* #129 (December 1972).

That's when I find the Trapster's tracking device hidden in my clothes. No wonder the rest of the Frightful Four found me so quickly! Argh! I crunch the computer chip in my grip and swing into action.

ZZZZZWAP!

WATCH WHERE YOU POINT THAT THING, IT MIGHT GO OFF!

I attack the Klaw first, shooting a web line at his sonic cannon and redirecting its pulse—straight back at him. Momentarily disoriented, the criminal conks his cranium on a column and crumples to the floor.

The Wizard's first appearance was in *Strange Tales* #102 (November 1962).

Then I somersault across the cafeteria toward Thundra and slam her into the lunch counter.

HEY, LITTLE MISS MUFFET, THIS SPIDER JUST KICKED YOUR TUFFET!

BAM!

The Wizard
organized
and is the
leader of the
Frightful Four.

Wizard uses his antigravity disks to launch the lunch tables into the air. He throws them all right at me, but I hop, skip, and jump over them.

LOOKS LIKE I'M OFF TO SEE THE WIZARD!

As I fight with Wizard, I remember what Nick Fury said about minding my surroundings. I need to get this terrible trio away from the civilians.

His real name
is Bentley
Wittman.

TIME TO SQUASH THIS BUG!

I sprint out of the hole in the wall and shoot my web line at the nearest building. The villains give chase. I'm clear across the rooftops when I get blasted by the Klaw's sonic cannon. Thundra whips her chain around my ankle and slams me into a brick wall. Ouch!

Klaw was a physicist who created a device that could turn sound into physical objects.

FWOOM!

Then Wizard and Klaw double-team me. Double ouch! I feel weak and fall down. Wizard comes over to check if I'm unconscious—but I surprise him with a solid kick to the solar plexus.

WHAM!

PEEKABOO!

His entire body has been replaced with solid sound that he can fire in concussive blasts.

15

Thundra runs over to the large water tank and rips the lid off with her bare hands. Just as she's about to crush this spider, Power Man appears and knocks it out of her hands.

YOU DROPPED SOMETHING!

Whoa, talk about perfect timing! Thundra fights back and throws my new ally into the water tower, tipping it over. Water splashes down, knocking the warrior woman off the ledge. I ride the waves down to catch her with my webbing.

SURF'S UP!

WHOOSH!

16

Wizard strikes next. He attaches an antigravity disk to Power Man and lifts him off his feet. Then the Wizard threatens to drop him to the ground below.

YO, SOMEBODY PLEASE CANCEL THIS ORDER OF STREET PIZZA!

SURRENDER NOW OR FALL TO YOUR DOOM!

Just then, Nova rockets onto the scene, and destroys the antigravity disk with a blast of cosmic energy. Power Man falls, but I save him in the nick of time.

Wizard blasts Nova with his energy beams but the rocketeer fires back. There is a brilliant burst of light, and seconds later, Wizard is flat on his back in the center of a smoking crater.

With Wizard down for the count, the Klaw blasts his sonic cannon at me again. Out of nowhere, White Tiger jumps on the villain's back with catlike agility. She holds him long enough for another ally to strike. It's Iron Fist, and he packs a big punch!

NOW THE SCREAM OF CHAOS WILL MEET THE SOUL OF IRON.

An earth-shattering sonic boom knocks Klaw off the building. I snatch him with my webbing and truss him up tight. Power Man crunches Klaw's cannon like a tin can. Cool.

LET'S CUT THE VOLUME!

Iron Fist first appeared in *Marvel Premiere* #15 (May 1974).

CRUNCH!

When banded together under the leadership of Spider-Man, these young heroes are known as the New Warriors.

Suddenly, the Helicarrier appears overhead and a group of S.H.I.E.L.D. agents bring the villains into custody. The young heroes invite me aboard and I find out they are actually S.H.I.E.L.D.'s newest recruits!

Iron Fist
Kung Fu master with a fist of iron.

Power Man
Superstrong fighter with bulletproof skin.

White Tiger
Acrobatic ninja with steel claws and cat powers.

Nova
The human rocket with cosmic-power abilities.

Then I discover from Agent Coulson that I'm being recruited to join the team, too. Possibly even lead them in battle. I think of Uncle Ben and how he once told me that "with great power comes great responsibility." I'm not ready for this. It's too much pressure!

NO WAY. I DIDN'T SIGN UP FOR A TEAM!

IT'S NOT A TEAM. IT'S A PROGRAM.

The Helicarrier is capable of independent flight.

I CAN'T BE RESPONSIBLE FOR A BUNCH OF ROOKIES.

It is the headquarters of S.H.I.E.L.D.

I WOULDN'T HAVE MADE THIS OFFER TO YOU OR THEM IF I DIDN'T SEE THE POTENTIAL FOR YOU TO BECOME THE NEXT GREAT TEAM. THE NEXT AVENGERS! THOSE KIDS HAVE THE TRAINING AND YOU HAVE THE REAL-WORLD EXPERIENCE. YOU ALL HAVE MUCH TO LEARN FROM EACH OTHER. THEY'RE WILLING TO GIVE YOU A CHANCE. WILL YOU GIVE THEM A CHANCE?

I think of how important it is to protect the people I care about most. It would honor my Uncle Ben's memory if I reached my maximum potential as a Super Hero by training with the experts. I accept Nick Fury's offer.

WELCOME TO S.H.I.E.L.D. HOPE YOU SURVIVE THE EXPERIENCE!

So, here I am. On the S.H.I.E.L.D. Helicarrier, being taught by the greatest superspy of all, Nick Fury. The training sequence begins and, after two seconds, the robots toss me around like a rag doll. How lame is that? I'm gonna end up on the wall of shame for dying ten minutes after joining S.H.I.E.L.D.

The good news is, they gave my web shooters an upgrade with S.H.I.E.L.D. tech and I use it to smash the robots into each other. Once I get into the swing of things, I whip those big hunks of junk into scrap metal.

THIS IS IT! THE TEST TO SEE IF I CAN MAKE IT IN THE SUPER HERO BIG LEAGUES.

THIS EXERCISE WILL GAUGE YOUR EFFICIENCY AGAINST SUPERIOR NUMBERS. YOU HAVE SIXTY SECONDS. CAPTAIN AMERICA MADE IT IN TEN.

SMASH!

EASY PEASY.

The next day at school, I try to act like everything is normal. All I can think about is how cool it was to train with S.H.I.E.L.D. agents. Suddenly, my Spider-Sense goes off and that big bully Flash Thompson is about to shove me in my locker—again.

OH, PUNY PARKER! IT'S LOCKER KNOCKER TIME!

A powerful hand grabs Flash and gives him a taste of his own medicine. I turn around to thank whomever helped me and he is with a group of teens that seem familiar. Finally, a light bulb goes off in my head and I make the connection!

DO I KNOW YOU GUYS?

THINK ABOUT IT.

WE'RE YOUR NEW CLASSMATES.

NO WAY!

Doctor Octopus first appeared in *The Amazing Spider-Man* #3 (July 1963).

Time passes and I grow closer to my new crew. We train together, hang out together, and sometimes save New York City when it's in danger. Today is one of those days, so we're doing what we do best: kicking bad guy butt! And this bad guy, Doctor Octopus, is especially nasty.

YOU AND THOSE BRATS ARE NO MATCH FOR ME, SPIDER-MAN!

EVERYONE GRAB AN ARM AND SHOW HIM SOME LOVE.

SLASH!

RIIIIIIP!

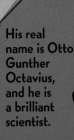

His real name is Otto Gunther Octavius, and he is a brilliant scientist.

Power Man grips one of Doc Ock's tentacles and uses his brute strength to rip it off. White Tiger slices right through another one with her steel claws.

Iron Fist shatters a third to pieces. And Nova puts on the finishing touch with an energy blast, knocking Doc Ock into a bus.

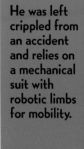

He was left crippled from an accident and relies on a mechanical suit with robotic limbs for mobility.

SHOOM!

SHRAK!

I shoot my webs at the dangerous doctor and yank him out of his armored suit. Then we tie him up tight and the day is saved!

The four robotic limbs, plus his arms and legs, give Doc Ock eight appendages like an octopus.

THWIP! THWIP!

OTTO, YOU NEED TO GET OUT MORE!

25

The Quinjet is a high-tech mode of transportation. It is a vertical take-off and landing aircraft with turbojet engines that can reach Mach 2.

While all this is happening, the actual Avengers are secretly watching us from their Quinjet and discussing my potential.

THE KID'S A NATURAL LEADER.

HE'S RISKY AND RECKLESS. I LIKE HIM!

BETTER THAN THAT. HE'S GOT HEART.

HE HAS A WARRIOR'S CUNNING!

The Avengers first appeared in *Avengers* #1 (September 1963).

Fury had mentioned they were interested in me, but I didn't think I was ever going to hear from them. And on this day of days, the Earth's Mightiest Heroes invite me to become a member of their team! Needless to say, my friends and I are in shock.

This is a tough decision and I am torn between two awesome teams. Leaving my old team is gonna be hard, but I make my choice and go with the Avengers. I follow them onto the Quinjet and IT IS AMAZING!

Spider-Man joined The Avengers in issue #316 (April 1990).

The Avengers are made up of several amazing and powerful members. They are Captain America, Iron Man, Hulk, Thor, Black Widow, Hawkeye, and Falcon.

Iron Man

Wears suit made of high-tech armor that he created, containing advanced weapons and technology.

Captain America

Supersoldier from World War II. Has enhanced strength, agility, and speed along with an indestructible shield.

Hulk

Gamma-powered superhuman. Giant in size, strength, speed, and endurance, with thick green skin and anger issues.

Black Widow

Special agent and superspy. Highly trained martial artist and gymnast with enhanced physical and mental attributes.

Falcon

Technology and science expert. Genius level intelligence with winged battle suit for aerial assaults.

Hawkeye

Skilled combatant and marksman. This archer's arsenal contains a bow with numerous trick arrows.

Thor

Warrior prince of Asgard who wields a mighty magical hammer and is invulnerable and nearly immortal.

Upon arriving at the Avengers tower, Jarvis directs me to a private room. I remind myself not to act like a clueless newbie! "Avengers Spidey" is cool and confident on the outside–but geeking out big-time on the inside!

Whoa! Suddenly, and without warning, I'm attacked from every direction by these mean machines. Looks like this is another training exercise. I'm so over them.

ZAZZAKK!

I'M JUST GETTING WARMED UP!

He inherited Stark Industries when he was just 21 years old.

Time to show this team what Spidey's all about. Big robots? I'm cool. Weird nasty fork thingies? I got this! Come on! Who's next?

Iron Man's first appearance was in *Tales of Suspense* #39 (March 1963).

Hawkeye's first appearance was in *Tales of Suspense* #57 (September 1964).

Just then, Tony Stark, the billionaire brains behind this little welcome party, walks into the room. Joining him are Hawkeye and Black Widow. It's a little unnerving to be in their presence, but I'm chill about it.

HEY, HAWKEYE. SPIDER-MAN BEAT YOUR TIME BY THREE SECONDS.

DUMB LUCK.

Black Widow's first appearance was in *Tales of Suspense* #52 (April 1964).

My head is still spinning from the pure awesomeness of having my own Avengers ID when Tony shares some new Avengers tech with me. He gives my web shooters a much-needed upgrade with complete access to an Avengers-only frequency.

YOU TREAT ALL YOUR NEW MEMBERS THIS WAY?

YES. YES WE DO. NO HARD FEELINGS. HERE'S YOUR OFFICIAL AVENGERS I.D.

THE SUPER HEROES ALL-ACCESS PASS! WHOO!

CAREFUL YOU DON'T SET OFF THE TASERS!

ARE THERE ANY OTHER SURPRISES I SHOULD KNOW ABOUT?

Hulk's first appearance was in *The Incredible Hulk* #1 (May 1962).

HULK NOOGIE WELCOME PATROL!! NOOGIE, NOOGIE, NOOGIE!

I'M SORRY I ASKED.

33

That night, in the holding cells on the Helicarrier, a magical figure manifests in the darkness. It is Loki, Thor's brother, and the wicked god of mischief! He pays Doctor Octopus an unexpected visit.

WHAT WOULD THE PRINCE OF TRICKSTERS WANT WITH A HUMBLE SCIENTIST LIKE ME?

I PLAN ON HUMILIATING THOR AND DESTROYING THE AVENGERS, INCLUDING ITS NEWEST MEMBER, SPIDER-MAN. WE CAN SQUASH THE BUG TOGETHER!

WHAT IS MY ROLE IN ALL THIS?

Loki helps Doc Ock escape, and they teleport beneath the island of Manhattan. Then Loki conjures up an Asgardian suit of armor for the fugitive to wear.

On Asgard, Earth is known as Midgard.

I'M INTRIGUED BY YOUR VENOM INVENTION. I'LL UNLEASH IT UPON THE MOST FEARSOME MONSTERS IN THE NINE REALMS!

I CREATED VENOM USING SPIDER-MAN'S BLOOD AND I'M FRESH OUT.

YOU NEED SPIDER-MAN'S BLOOD? LEAVE THAT TO ME!

Venom is the name of a symbiote, or living organism that attaches itself to a host, forming an almost unstoppable weapon.

35

Hulk's alias is Dr. Bruce Banner, a scientist caught in an explosion of gamma radiation that transformed him into a green goliath.

The next day, my new teammate, Hulk, wants to go to an all-you-can-eat buffet. He comes looking for me but I hide so he doesn't find me. To be honest, being an Avenger rocks—but I can't handle any more of the big guy's gut-busting activities.

I need some Spidey alone time and there's nothing better than a nice, relaxing swing over the city.

Then, BAM! I'm blindsided by a mystical bolt of green energy. Ouch!

NOW THAT'S HOW I LIKE A SPIDER...SQUIRMING, HELPLESS, AND ABOUT TO BE CRUSHED!

Loki's first appearance was in Venus #6 (1949).

Loki! This dude is bad news. I pull out my ID and hope that it has some sort of Avengers Alert. Just then, Loki zaps it out of my hands, deactivating it.

Acting fast, I shoot webbing to the wall above and pull a chunk of rock onto Loki's head. KLONK! It barely fazes him! Guess that helmet is a lot stronger than it looks.

SMASH!

OKAY, PAL. IT'S LIGHTS-OUT FOR YOU!

ON THE CONTRARY, SPIDER-MAN. YOU ARE GETTING... WEARY...SLEEPY. GO TO SLEEP.

He blasts me clear across the city back into the Avengers Tower. My head gets all fuzzy and everything goes black.

Spiders are arachnids. There are 40,000 species of spider, most of them harmless to humans.

Spiders create webs out of silk to catch their prey. Abandoned spiderwebs are called cobwebs.

Meanwhile, in the secret underwater lab, Doc Ock receives another visit from an even more unexpected guest. The doctor attacks in a fit of rage but the guest is far more than meets the eye.

YOU! AARGH!

IT'S ME, FOOL! I PROMISED YOU SPIDER-MAN'S BODY, SO HERE IT IS.

LOKI? YOU PUT YOUR MIND IN SPIDER-MAN'S BODY? THAT'S BRILLIANT! I'M GONNA WRITE THAT DOWN.

INDEED. TO NEW YORK'S HORRIFIED EYES, IT WON'T BE LOKI LEADING AN INVASION OF MONSTERS AGAINST THE AVENGERS, BUT THEIR NEWEST MEMBER, SPIDER-MAN!

I wake up with a pounding headache and take in my surroundings. My body feels funny and that's when I realize—it's not mine! It's Loki's!

Okay, the most important thing is not to panic. I have to explain to the others what happened before they smash me. Uh-oh...

NO, NO, NO, NO, NO! THIS CAN'T BE HAPPENING.

LOKI? HULK SMASH!

CRASH!

Vice versa is a latin phrase meaning "the other way around."

The green goliath punches me right through a wall and I find myself inside a training room with Captain America, Hawkeye, and Black Widow. This is not going to end well.

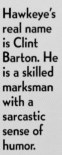

Hawkeye's real name is Clint Barton. He is a skilled marksman with a sarcastic sense of humor.

Hawkeye strikes quickly, hitting me square in the chest with an exploding arrow. Cap follows suit with his shield, knocking me in the head, and Widow kicks me across the room.

LOOK AT THAT. TARGET PRACTICE!

CHOOM!

NO, WAIT, NO! OOF!

Black Widow's real name is Natasha Romanoff. She is an expert martial artist.

To top it all off, Iron Man appears and blasts me through the roof.

As if things couldn't get worse, I land right in front of Thor. I plead with him to hear me out, but he pounds me with his magic hammer and I go sailing straight into the Daily Bugle's digital billboard. This is totally not my day.

Thor's first appearance was in *Venus* #12 (1951).

FINALLY. IF ANYONE CAN TELL I'M NOT THE REAL LOKI, IT'S YOU, RIGHT?!

MORE TRICKERY FROM THE PRINCE OF LIES! BE GONE!

Spider-Man's first appearance was in *Amazing Fantasy* #15 (August 1962).

BUT I'M REALLY SPIDER-MAAAAAAAAAAAN!

Meanwhile, live news footage is shocking. New York is swarming with monsters that look like they're covered in Venom! So that's what horn-head is up to. He's wrecking the city and setting me up to take the fall! This needs to end now. I command Loki's staff to fly me to my body, but I fall flat on my face.

LOKI DOESN'T FLY? I THOUGHT HE FLEW.

THUMP!

My only option is to take public transportation. I catch a bus and once I enter, I get stares from the other passengers. Even for New York City, I look pretty weird.

WHAT? I'M GOING TO A COMIC CONVENTION. THIS IS MY STOP!

Suddenly, the bus screeches to a halt and a Thor-sized wolf covered in Venom tears its way in. There's only one man who can create Venom for Loki, and I'm thinking this Asgardian rat is working with an Earth octopus.

The creature attacks me and I defend myself with Loki's scepter. I'm not sure how this thing works, but if it protects Loki, it must protect me, right? A green beam of energy blasts the beast unconscious.

New York Comic Con was first held in 2006 at the Jacob K. Javits Convention Center.

ZAP!

The first Avengers to respond are Falcon, Thor, and Hulk. The winged warrior shoots his flechettes at a vicious Venom-laced dragon, slicing through its symbiotic suit. Then Hulk leaps into action and punches the dragon out.

BAM!

I HAD NO IDEA SPIDER-MAN HAD SO MUCH POWER...AND WAS SO DELIBERATELY EVIL!

HE'S NOT, FALCON. WE ACTED TOO RASHLY. THIS INVASION IS LOKI'S PLOT!

THIS BLACK ICE CHILLS MY SOUL!

KA-THOOM!

Thor's hammer is called Mjolnir, pronounced Me-YOL-neer. It means "that which smashes" (much like the Incredible Hulk).

Thor calls down the lightning with his hammer and blasts a bunch of beasts. Another dragon attacks and spits Venom at Hulk and Thor. The magical substance freezes quickly and traps the heroes in place!

HARD TO CONTROL AND HARD TO SMASH!

Mjolnir is made of an indestructible metal and is enchanted so that only Thor can pick it up.

The maniac behind this mayhem enjoys watching Thor and his friends suffer. He cackles with glee and tries to get closer to the action— but isn't very successful. Guess it takes a real Spider-Man to swing with style.

GLORIOUS! LET FLY, WEB!

OOF. IDIOTIC MORTAL CONTRAPTION. THIS IS A SURPRISINGLY LABORIOUS PROCESS. AM I SWEATING? DISGUSTING! THAT STENCH! DOESN'T HE WASH THIS RIDICULOUS COSTUME?

Finally, I catch up to the trickster and give him a taste of his own medicine—with a sucker punch right in the gut! WHUP!

IT'S A TWO-FOR-ONE DEAL. I'M GOING TO SEND YOU AND MY SUIT TO THE CLEANERS!

YOU FOOL, YOU'RE ONLY HURTING YOURSELF!

Loki doesn't laugh at my joke. Probably because he doesn't find it funny. Well, he is Asgardian. He probably has laundry gnomes wash his clothes.

AVENGERS, IT'S ME, SPIDER-MAN! STOP LOKI BEFORE HE GETS AWAY!

ZZZACKKK!

The two of us struggle for control of Loki's scepter, when, suddenly, there is a blinding flash of light. Loki has switched our bodies back to normal and I double over in pain. AARGH! He's right—I gave my own body a beating and now everything hurts. And it gets worse as soon as my teammates arrive.

He likes to trade quips and "THWIPS!"

Some spiders can swim. The diving bell spider is the only spider that actually lives underwater.

When I joined the Avengers, I never thought they would attack me! Jumping as fast as I can, I try to avoid their aerial assault. I have to find a way to convince them that I'm really Spider-Man before I get clobbered!

HURRY AND SMITE HIM BEFORE HE CASTS ANOTHER SPELL!

My only choice is to leap into the river and swim to safety. SPLASH! I swim for a while until I make my way into the sewers. If my suit didn't smell rancid before, it certainly does now. Gross! Luckily, I am close to where I can find help–Midtown High!

The East River is not really a river! It is a saltwater tidal strait that connects upper New York Bay to Long Island Sound.

YIKES!

I search for my S.H.I.E.L.D. crew and find them already suited up. They are receiving a transmission from Nick Fury—which prompts them to chase me down the hall!

AN ARMY OF VENOMIZED MONSTERS HAS ALREADY TAKEN OUT HULK AND THOR. AND WITH LOKI INSIDE SPIDER-MAN'S BODY, HE'S A BIGGER THREAT THAN BEFORE!

HEY SPIDEY PALS...UH, MAYBE THIS WAS A BAD TIME TO DROP IN?

IT'S LOKI! GET HIM!

Iron Fist pounds the tile, sending the force of an earthquake at me. I flip onto the lockers to avoid it, but Power Man is there in no time trying to use me as a punching bag. Gotta move fast!

GAME OVER, TRICKSTER!

WAIT! I'M REALLY ME! I'M SPIDER-MAN!

WHAM!

White Tiger slashes at the lockers and nearly makes minced spider out of me. No one wants to listen, so I'll have to prove my identity by revealing something only the true Spider-Man would know.

NOVA! I KNOW YOU'RE SECRETLY AFRAID OF BUNNIES!

HEY! UH...I MEAN, NO I'M NOT!

Nova hits me with his energy blasts. Ouch, those things hurt! I refuse to fight back, hoping that it proves my innocence. Nova's fist stops an inch from my face!

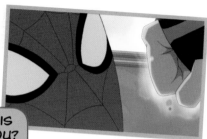

Iron Fist takes himself very seriously and is the most calm member of the group. He likes to practice staying Zen unless it's time for battle.

DID THE PURITY OF HIS ACTIONS CONVINCE YOU?

PURITY NOTHING! THE REAL LOKI WOULD NEVER TRAVEL BY SEWER! BLECCH!

He is a master of the K'un-Lun's martial arts.

Suddenly, the wall explodes and the Avengers appear–with Loki in the lead!

LOKI MUST BE CONTROLLING THEIR MINDS. ATTACK!

YOU HEARD THE MAN. LETS DO IT!

Iron Fist pounds the ground again, knocking the Avengers off balance. This gives us enough time to escape. Nova scoops me up and we blast off down the hall.

In seconds, we clear the school yard and land near the elevated subway train.

KA-POW!

WE HAVE TO GET YOU OUT OF HERE.

Power Man received his amazing abilities from a serum.

YO, WHAT'S OUR BATTLE PLAN?

DUDE, I DON'T KNOW. THEY'RE THE AVENGERS. HIT 'EM HARD AND TRY TO WIN!

THAT'S A TERRIBLE PLAN!

It seems like Bucket Head is trying to lead the team when I'm not around. It's time to put my leadership skills to the test and show them how it's done!

Despite his incredible strength, he is very soft-spoken and immensely loyal to his friends.

WHITE TIGER, YOU TAKE BLACK WIDOW. IRON FIST, YOU'RE ON HAWKEYE. POWER MAN, FORCE IRON MAN'S ARMOR TO REBOOT BY HITTING IT WITH SOMETHING BIG. NOVA AND I WILL PICK UP THE REST.

ON IT!

Iron Man's arc reactor powers his armor. It also keeps a piece of lodged shrapnel from entering Tony's heart.

While White Tiger and Iron Fist keep the superspy and archer busy, I distract Iron Man long enough for Power Man to make his move. Suddenly, an empty truck hurtles toward the armored Avenger. He uses his arc reactor to force it away, accidentally smashing the support beam of nearby train tracks. A train car full of people comes tumbling down!

CRASH!

I rush to grab it, but the strain is too great! I think that's when the Avengers reboot their opinion of me.

A LITTLE HELP HERE, GUYS.

LOKI WOULD NEVER SAVE INNOCENT VICTIMS. WE GOT THE WRONG GUY!

Some jumping spiders can lift more than 100 times their length.

54

Iron Man and Captain America join me in placing the train car gently on the ground. Thanks to our teamwork, the citizens are safe. Captain America is even impressed with my skills.

Captain America's real name is Steve Rogers.

HEY, YOU'RE A GOOD LEADER.

LOOK, SORRY FOR THE MIX UP.

IT HELPS TO HAVE A GOOD TEAM! NOW LET'S GO HELP HULK AND THOR.

Steve was injected with the Super Soldier Serum which immediately increased his body mass, strength, speed, and agility.

Then I say what I've been dying to say since I joined the team:

AVENGERS, ASSEMBLE!

In nature, venom is a substance that some creatures inject into their victims to stun, kill, or even help digest prey from the inside out!

The Avengers and my S.H.I.E.L.D. crew will need to combine forces against these menacing monsters. When we find Hulk and Thor, they are guarded by a host of creatures. The monsters shoot liquid Venom at us, but Captain America uses his shield as protection.

OKAY, AVENGERS. LET'S DO THIS!

Black Widow attacks using her patented "Widow's Bites." They are high-frequency electrostatic charges that can deliver up to 30,000 volts!

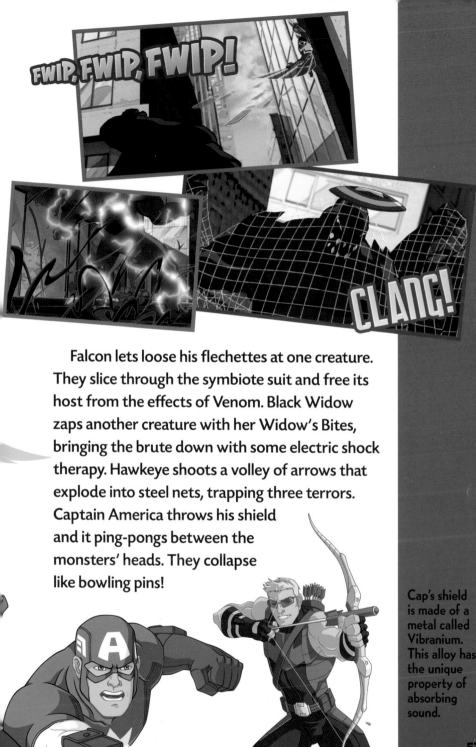

FWIP, FWIP, FWIP!

CLANG!

Falcon lets loose his flechettes at one creature. They slice through the symbiote suit and free its host from the effects of Venom. Black Widow zaps another creature with her Widow's Bites, bringing the brute down with some electric shock therapy. Hawkeye shoots a volley of arrows that explode into steel nets, trapping three terrors. Captain America throws his shield and it ping-pongs between the monsters' heads. They collapse like bowling pins!

Cap's shield is made of a metal called Vibranium. This alloy has the unique property of absorbing sound.

Falcon's real name is Sam Wilson. He is gifted in physical sciences, much like his mentor, Tony Stark.

Meanwhile, Iron Man and Nova use their energy blasts to free Hulk and Thor, while Power Man and Iron Fist aid in chipping away at the frozen substance with their punches.

HEY GUYS, LET'S GIVE THEM A HAND!

WHAM! BAM! CRASH!

I flip over one of the creatures and notice he is wielding a Venomized ice club. I nimbly hop out of his way as he swings and misses. One of my swift kicks knocks him over but I land right into the path of a big, bad Venom-wolf. A Venom tendril wraps my ankle and pulls me into his chomping maw.

Falcon's suit lets him fly at incredible speeds using holographic wings that can shoot explosive projectiles called flechettes.

Falcon's first appearance was in *Captain America* #117 (September 1969).

All of a sudden, a forceful wind from Falcon's wings blows off the symbiote suit and reveals the Asgardian wolf beneath. Now vulnerable, he falls prey to my upgraded Avengers-tech web-taser.

IT'S BEDTIME, BIG BAD!

ZZZARK!

The Venom symbiote is highly sensitive to extreme heat and can disintegrate in its presence.

Hawkeye follows suit and shoots heated arrows at the monsters. They melt the Venom away, revealing more Asgardian adversaries. I zap them both before they cause any more damage.

WHAT DID YOU DO TO MY LITTLE PAL!

FSSSSSS!

ZZZARK!

Before joining the Avengers, Clint Barton was a carnival acrobat and archer known as Hawkeye the Marksman.

Finally, Hulk and Thor are free–except they don't know I'm really me!

His arsenal contains a variety of trick arrows that both defeat and humiliate his foes.

IT'S REALLY SPIDER-MAN. LOKI SWITCHED THEM BACK.

GOOD TO HAVE YOU BACK!

Hulk gives me a pat on the back that nearly sends me to New Jersey.

UGH...LOVE HURTS.

The Venom symbiote is also sensitive to concussive sound.

At that very moment, a second wave of Venom monsters comes down Broadway. New Yorkers flee in every direction. Captain America attacks them first.

HIT 'EM HIGH, LOW, AND EVERYWHERE ELSE!

WHAP!

The supersoldier delivers a right jab and a roundhouse kick to the nearest creature.

Black Widow jumps on the back of another. She shocks it with her Widow's Bites.

Hawkeye is surrounded by several of them, but he takes each one down with well-aimed exploding arrows.

DON'T CROWD. I HAVE ENOUGH ARROWS FOR EVERYONE.

ZAP!

FWOOM!

Power Man grabs one by the tongue and pulls its face into his fist. The symbiote recoils from the pain, revealing the Asgardian host beneath.

WHOA, AND I THOUGHT THEY WERE UGLY ON THE OUTSIDE!

POW!

Iron Man blasts the oncoming threat with a concussive sound cannon. Now stripped of their alien parasite, the creatures are easily taken out by Iron Fist, Power Man, White Tiger, and Nova.

THE SYMBIOTE IS SENSITIVE TO SOUND. I'VE CONVERTED MY REPULSOR RAYS TO SONIC WAVES!

CHOOM! CHOOM! CHOOM!

Pigeons fly an average of 50 miles per hour, and as fast as 90 miles per hour.

The third wave of Venom monsters attacks from above. Now that he's free, Hulk is itching to smash something. He leaps over the buildings and lands on the flying creature's back.

BLASTED NEW YORK PIGEONS! THEY GET BIGGER EVERY TIME!

New York City alone has an estimated pigeon population of over 1 million birds!

Thor thunders into battle behind the green goliath. He clashes his mighty hammer against the ice swords of a Frost Giant and shatters them into icicles. Then he commands his comrade back on Asgard to create an interdimensional portal.

Together, Thor and Hulk begin hurling the monsters back to their place of origin.

The Bifrost is a magic link between all the Nine Realms of the Norse cosmos.

> HEIMDALL! OPEN THE BIFROST.

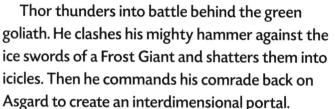

It is guarded and operated by Heimdall, a Norse warrior.

SHRRRAK!

The first closed-circuit scuba suit was designed and built by English diving engineer Henry Fleuss in 1878.

The rest of the Avengers, along with the S.H.I.E.L.D. team, take turns hurling monsters into the Bifrost. And yes, it is as fun as it looks.

Incoming call from Director Fury! Excuse me, I gotta take this.

BREEP! BREEP!

ENERGY READINGS SHOW THAT DOC OCK'S OLD UNDERWATER LAB IS UP AND RUNNING AGAIN.

MY OLD TEAM AND I WILL GO FLUSH HIM OUT SINCE WE'VE DEALT WITH THE DOC BEFORE.

The good news about our new mission? We get S.H.I.E.L.D.-issued scuba gear that is way cool! The bad news? Another dip inside New York's East River. BLECH!

We follow Fury's coordinates and swim deep down to the lab. Inside, there is a big vat of Venom. Our objective is to destroy it and stop the Doc!

READY FOR ROUND TWO? MY NEW ARMOR WAS CONSTRUCTED BY LOKI'S DARKEST MAGIC!

Uh-oh! Looks like someone has gotten some upgrades of his own since we last met. White Tiger, Power Man, Iron Fist, and I leap into action. We tackle the tentacles while Nova blasts the vat with a beam of cosmic energy, eradicating all traces of Venom.

CHOOM!

NO!

It can take a very long time for a spider to drown because its body uses very little oxygen.

Fuming with rage, Doc Ock rips off our scuba masks with his mechanical arms. Then he tears apart the structure, flooding the lab. The water is rising quickly and we need to get out!

IT'S TIME TO WASH THIS SPIDER OUT!

ONE WEB-BALL SPECIAL TO GO!

The octopus is considered the most intelligent of all invertebrates.

Acting fast, I build a protective web cocoon around my teammates and order Nova to blast us out of there fast!

Meanwhile, Dr. Octopus extends his tentacles until he is towering over the East River like a sinister sea monster. Before he can strike, my friends and I break the surface of the water.

Octopi have well developed senses and enormous brains for their size.

WHAT DOES IT TAKE TO DROWN YOU, SPIDER-MAN?

INTERESTING QUESTION.

Before we find out the answer, a crackle of electricity fills the air and Thor appears to confront Doc Ock.

Thor fights the demented doctor, but his blows bounce off the Asgardian armor.

HOLD, MAN OF OCTOPI! SURRENDER FOR YOUR OWN SAKE!

KRA-KOOM!

Across town, Loki watches the events unfold from atop Avengers Tower—which he has magically rebuilt in his image. I've seen a lot of crazy things in this city, but that is just nasty!

Loki enjoys seeing his brother get thrashed, but he does not enjoy the Avengers defeating his Venom army.

OTTO! THOSE FOOLS ARE DESTROYING OUR CREATIONS. ATTACK THEM!

The tentacled terror lumbers down an avenue straight into the thick of battle. Iron Man flies at his side and tries to reason with him. He tells Otto he will ultimately be betrayed because Loki is dishonest and cruel.

YOU DO KNOW THAT HIS JOB DESCRIPTION IS PRINCE OF LIES, RIGHT?

SHUT YOUR YAMMERING TRAP, STARK!

It has jet-boot-powered flight.

Doc Ock attempts to crush the armored Avenger, but Tony zigs and zags and zooms far faster than his octopus-like opponent.

The armor can fire high-energy repulsor beams from the gauntlets and chest as well as rocket missiles from the shoulders, back, and wrists.

WELL, I TRIED REASON. HERE'S PLAN B.

A volley of rockets launch from the hidden panels inside Iron Man's armor. That dude has definitely got style. But the missiles are deflected by Otto's Asgardian armor. Doc Ock grabs Iron Man in his grasp and slams him into Hulk.

WHAM!

Originally a dull gray, Tony's armor is red and gold, reflecting his colorful personality.

An octopus has eight appendages called tentacles.

I distract the doctor by leading him on a merry chase away from my teammates. This time, I try to put Tony's brilliant plan into effect by talking to Doc Ock and convincing him that he is being used by Loki as a mere pawn.

HEY! WHY DON'T YOU PICK ON SOMEONE YOUR OWN SIZE?

Doc Ock pauses to think as Loki enters the fray, facing off against the Avengers and my S.H.I.E.L.D. crew. Thor blasts Loki with a bolt of electricity.

IT GRIEVES ME THAT WE MUST BATTLE AGAIN, BROTHER.

ZZZZARK!

Loki zaps Doc Ock with the staff to get his attention. Bad idea. Well, bad for Loki, anyway. Good idea for us. Otto grabs Loki in his tentacle and threatens him.

I WILL NOT BE DEFEATED. OTTO, ASSIST ME NOW!

I AM NOT YOUR SERVANT! IT'S TIME TO END THIS PARTNERSHIP!

AN EXCELLENT SUGGESTION.

The angrier Hulk gets, the stronger he becomes.

Loki conjures another spell that encircles Otto in a swirling, glowing green mist. The trickster god strips Doc Ock of his Asgardian armor. The helpless henchman plummets through the air but I swing by and catch him. Just another service, courtesy of your friendly neighborhood Spider-Man!

THIS OCTOPUS IS HANGING OUT TO DRY.

Loki is now left to fend for himself. Hulk grabs the mischief-maker so he can't escape and now it's my turn to have some fun. Hey, payback isn't pretty! I tell Hulk he should be pals with Loki. The big guy thinks I'm nuts until the idea sinks in.

Hulk has extremely powerful legs and can leap great distances.

OH, YEAH. PALS! NOOGIE, NOOGIE, NOOGIE, NOOGIE, NOOGIE!

SURRENDER LOKI. YOU ARE NO MATCH FOR US NOW.

A noogie is a hard poke or grind with the knuckles, especially on a person's head.

The Avengers were formed when Loki came to Earth and tricked Hulk into causing a train wreck. Thor banded a group of Super Heroes together to stop Hulk and capture Loki.

I point to the portal and tell Loki to make a break for it. Whimpering, the cowardly conjurer rushes toward the Bifrost. Before he escapes, I wrap him up tight in my new souped-up webbing.

Hulk thinks I let him off easy, but Captain America and Thor understand the genius of my actions.

Captain America was not an original team member like Iron Man and Thor. He joined the Super Hero group in *Avengers* Volume 1, #4 (March 1964).

SMART PLAN, KID.

FOOLISH LOKI! LEAPS BEFORE HE LOOKS.

The Bifrost portal didn't lead back to Asgard—but into the parallel dimension where we sent the monsters! Loki is now trapped with the very creatures he had tricked. They are angry and they have a score to settle. I wish him luck—or NOT!

It's nighttime now in New York City and the two teams are parting ways. The Avengers head to their tower just as the Helicarrier arrives. I have to make a choice which way to go.

Agents of S.H.I.E.L.D. take Doc Ock aboard the aircraft. My old teammates follow.

IT WAS GREAT WORKING TOGETHER JUST LIKE THE GOOD OLD DAYS. BUT...UH...I'M AN AVENGER NOW.

YOU'RE A GREAT LEADER, MAN. I'M PROUD TO KNOW YOU.

REMEMBER, IT'S NOT THE DESTINATION THAT DEFINES YOU, BUT THE JOURNEY.

Before I say good-bye to my friends, I feel a hand on my shoulder. I turn to see Iron Man.

That same year, a copy of *Amazing Fantasy* #15 sold at auction for a record-breaking 1.1 million dollars, making Spider-Man the ultimate collector's item!

> AVENGERS TOWER WILL ALWAYS BE HERE, SPIDEY. WHENEVER YOU WANT. I'M SURE WE'LL MANAGE UNTIL YOU COME BACK.

> IT'S GOOD TO BE HOME.

As the Armored avenger streaks across the night sky, I look back at my S.H.I.E.L.D. friends and decide to stay with them. I know that I made the right decision.

Uncle Ben said that with great power comes great responsibility. Being a Super Hero is certainly a roller-coaster ride. It has its ups and downs. Luckily, I don't have to go through it alone. I have my family and my friends as well as my S.H.I.E.L.D. crew and the Avengers!

They've helped me reach my potential. I am a good leader. I am a great Super Hero!

I AM ULTIMATE SPIDER-MAN!